The BEST Chip

Kate Leake

ALISON GREEN BOOKS

Chubble, chobble, chomp and chew,
Chubbling chips is fun to do.
Chips are why I'm in this queue.
I like chubbling chips, do you?

CHIPS
SERVED HERE

PECK

I'm the world's **Chip-Chubbling CHAMP!**
I'd chomp chips every day —
For breakfast, brunch and tea and lunch,
If I had things my way.

Chips are **chopped**
    and **chipped** and **cooked**
In many different ways.
They come in bags or last week's news,
On plates or paper trays.

Bendy chips and floppy chips,
Long and thin and stringy.
Some are fat and some are flat,
And some are BIG and springy.

Short and spiky spicy chips
Are crunchy as you munch.
But crispy-light and cooked-just-right chips
Make the perfect lunch.

I like chips in crispy coats,
With fluffy-soft inside.

Me, too!

And crinkly,
   wrinkly chips are nice,
With ketchup on the side.

SNIFF
SNIFF

Some chips are quite horrid, though,
Like those with big black eyes.

Or Granny's famous frazzled chips,
With charcoal chicken pies.

Greasy chips that lie in gutters,
Old and cold and smelly!

Chips in dumps all stuck in lumps,
With rotting raspberry jelly.

Dad likes chips that swim around
In green and gloopy slime.
How CAN he eat those sloppy peas?
I won't have mush on mine!

Just a squelchy splodge of sauce,
(But watch out as you squirt.)
Squeeze too hard and there it goes . . .

. . . splat!

All down Dad's clean shirt!

And save the **biggest** chips for last,
'Cos those ones are the best!

WOW!

That's a whopper! Look at that!

I've never seen a chip so . . .

It's taller than my strawberry milk,
It's taller than a tower.

SLURP!

This mighty, mammoth **monster** chip
Could give me **super power!**

It's longer than three dozen cars.

It's BIGGER than the planet Mars!

Mars

my chip

But which end should I start with first?

I'm so excited I could BURST!

My chip's the BEST, I know it is!
No one has a chip like this.
It's tip, it's top, too best to chop!
Everyone do the Best-Chip Hop . . .

Flip those fritters, flip them high,
Bop those burgers, pat that pie.
Groove that gravy, flirt and squirt . . .

More big stains on Dad's clean shirt!
Do the jumbo sausage jive,
And dance the dunkin' doughnut dive.

Lick those lips and chomp those chips,
Balance them on your nose like this . . .

Wobble, look out!
Oops!

Whoops . . .

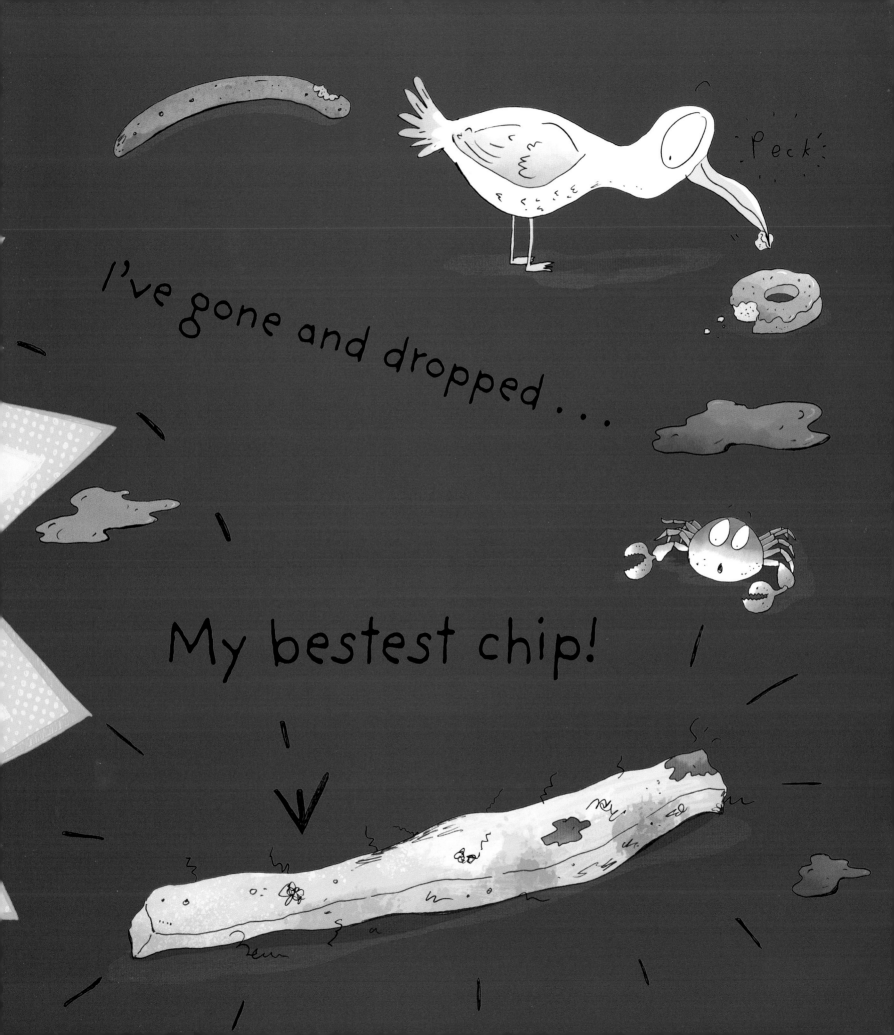

My **bestest** chip is on the floor!
Grimy, slimy, **best** no more.
It's hairy, black and sort of . . . flat.

I'd NEVER eat
a chip like that!

It was my chip, my perfect chip,
A better-than-the-rest best chip!
A chip that NEVER touched my tongue.

But no need to be sad for long . . .

'Cos I like chubbling chocolate cake,
With chocolate-chip ice cream.

It's better than the BESTEST chips . . .

. . . And chubbles like a dream!

SQUAWK!

For my super-brilliant Dad . . .
You're the BEST!
With love xxx

This edition first published in the UK in 2017 by
Alison Green Books
An imprint of Scholastic Children's Books
Euston House, 24 Eversholt Street,
London NW1 1DB
A division of Scholastic Ltd
www.scholastic.co.uk
London – New York – Toronto – Sydney – Auckland
Mexico City – New Delhi – Hong Kong
Original edition first published in 2006 by
Macmillan Children's Books

Copyright © 2006 & 2017 Kate Leake

ISBN: 978 1 407166 42 1

9 8 7 6 5 4 3 2